WITHDRAWN

A Note to Parents and Caregivers:

With a focus on math, science, and social studies, *Read-it!* Readers support both the learning of content information and the extension of more complex reading skills. They encourage the development of problem-solving skills that help children expand their thinking.

 The PURPLE LEVEL presents basic topics and objects using high frequency words and simple language patterns.

 The RED LEVEL presents familiar topics using common words and repeating sentence patterns.

 The BLUE LEVEL presents new ideas using a larger vocabulary and varied sentence structure.

 The YELLOW LEVEL presents more challenging ideas, a broad vocabulary, and wide variety in sentence structure.

 The GREEN LEVEL presents more complex ideas, an extended vocabulary range, and expanded language structures.

 The ORANGE LEVEL presents a wide range of ideas and concepts using challenging vocabulary and complex language structures.

When sharing a content focused book with your child, read to find out facts and concepts, pausing often to restate and talk about the new information. The realistic story format provides an opportunity to talk about the language used, and to learn about reading to problem-solve for information. Encourage children to measure, make maps, and consider other situations that allow them to apply what they are learning.

There is no right or wrong way to share books with children. Find time to read and share new learning with your child, and pass on the legacy of literacy.

Adria F. Klein, Ph.D.
Professor Emeritus
California State University
San Bernardino, California

Editor: Shelly Lyons
Designer: Abbey Fitzgerald
Page Production: Michelle Biedscheid
Art Director: Nathan Gassman
Associate Managing Editor: Christianne Jones
The illustrations in this book were created with acrylics.

Picture Window Books
151 Good Counsel Drive
P.O. Box 669
Mankato, MN 56002-0669
877-845-8392
www.picturewindowbooks.com

Printed in the United States of America.

Library of Congress Cataloging-in-Publication Data
Emerson, Carl.
The summer playground / by Carl Emerson ; illustrated by Cori Doerrfeld.
p. cm. — (Read-it! readers: Science)
ISBN 978-1-4048-2626-7 (library binding)
ISBN 978-1-4048-4757-6 (paperback)
1. Summer—Juvenile literature. I. Doerrfeld, Cori, ill. II. Title.
QB637.6.E44 2009
508.2—dc22   2008007167

The Summer Playground

by Carl Emerson
illustrated by Cori Doerrfeld

Special thanks to our advisers for their expertise:

Dr. Jon E. Ahlquist, Ph.D.
Department of Meteorology, Florida State University
Tallahassee, Florida

Adria F. Klein, Ph.D.
Professor Emeritus, California State University
San Bernardino, California

PiCTURE WiNDOW BOOKS
Minneapolis, Minnesota

Emma was going to meet Owen at the park.

Owen was on his way to the park. He saw yellow, red, and white flowers.

Summer was finally here!

In North America, summer begins in June and ends in September. The seasons of autumn, winter, and spring follow.

Emma and Owen met near Old Oak.

Old Oak was covered with bright green leaves.

During summer, the sun follows its highest path in the sky. This gives us more daylight hours. It also means temperatures in most places are higher.

The park had new swings and slides.

Emma and Owen could not wait
to play.

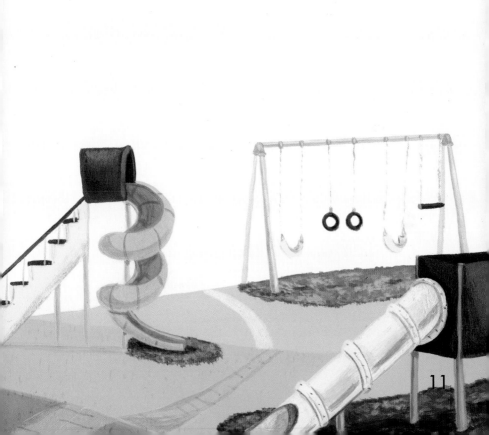

Just then, Rachel the robin came by.

"Today is a big day!" Rachel said.

13

"Yes, it is," said Emma.

"The new swings and slides are here!"
Owen said.

"But it may be too hot to play,"
Emma said.

"No, no," said Rachel. "We birds know how to keep cool."

"How do you stay cool?" Emma asked.

But Rachel was already flying away.

Emma and Owen wanted to play. They ran to the new swings and slides.

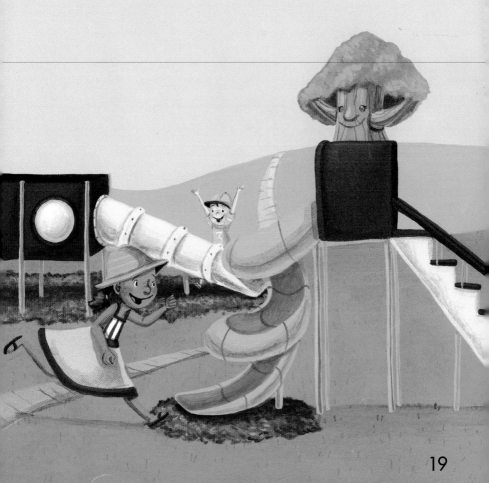

Soon the sun beat down on the kids.

"I'm really hot," said Emma.

People and animals need extra water when it is hot outside.

"Me, too," said Owen. "How does Rachel stay cool?"

The kids walked over to Old Oak.

"I don't know. What should we do?"
asked Emma.

They climbed Old Oak's branches.

Rachel was resting in her nest.

Emma and Owen could feel the cool shade from the leaves above.

Trees use their leaves to take in sunlight, water, and air. They also use their roots to take in water.

"I know how birds keep cool!"
said Emma.

"They find shade!" she said.

Too much sun is bad for your skin. It is important to protect your skin. Always wear sunscreen and a hat.

"You are right," said Old Oak. "I am always happy to help with that."

Fun Summer Activities

You can do many fun things in summer. Here are some ideas:

- Go to a local park and play on the playground.

- Go to a beach and make sand castles.

- Pack a picnic lunch. Find a large tree to sit under for its shade.

- Plant flowers or vegetables to celebrate the growing season.

- Go to a wooded area and search for animal paw prints. Take a picture of each print you find. Compare your pictures to images of paw prints on the Web. Try and figure out which animal made the print.

- Make your own nature museum. Build a collection of shells, twigs, pebbles, leaves, and interesting seeds. Display and label them for others to see.

- Check out a bird book at your local library. Use the book to discover what kinds of birds live in your area.

Glossary

season—one of the four parts of the year; winter, spring, summer, and autumn
summer—the season after spring and before autumn
sunscreen—lotion that protects skin from the harmful rays of the sun

To Learn More

More Books to Read

Glaser, Linda. *It's Summer!* Brookfield, Conn.: Millbrook Press, 2003.

Jackson, Ellen. *The Summer Solstice.* Brookfield, Conn.: Millbrook Press, 2001.

Low, Alice. *Summer.* New York: Random House, 2007.

Roca, Núria. *Summer.* Hauppauge, N.Y.: Barron's Educational Series, 2004.

On the Web

FactHound offers a safe, fun way to find Web sites related to topics in this book. All of the sites on FactHound have been researched by our staff.

1. Visit www.facthound.com
2. Type in this special code: 1404826262
3. Click on the FETCH IT button.

Your trusty FactHound will fetch the best sites for you!

Look for all of the books in the *Read-it!* Readers: Science series:

Friends and Flowers (life science: bulbs)
The Grass Patch Project (life science: grass)
The Sunflower Farmer (life science: sunflowers)
Surprising Beans (life science: beans)

The Moving Carnival (physical science: motion)
A Secret Matter (physical science: matter)
A Stormy Surprise (physical science: electricity)
Up, Up in the Air (physical science: air)

The Autumn Leaf (Earth science: seasons)
The Busy Spring (Earth science: seasons)
The Cold Winter Day (Earth science: seasons)
The Summer Playground (Earth science: seasons)